S0-BCU-389

POKéMON

Snack Attack!

MANVILLE PUBLIC LIBRARY
MANVILLE, NJ 08835

Adapted by
Tracey West

OFFICIAL
Pokémon
MASTER'S
CLUB

SCHOLASTIC INC.
New York Toronto London Auckland Sydney
Mexico City New Delhi Hong Kong Buenos Aires

MANVILLE PUBLIC LIBRARY
MANVILLE NJ 08835

© 2005 Pokémon.
© 1995–2005 Nintendo/Creatures Inc./GAME FREAK inc. TM & ® are trademarks of
Nintendo. All rights reserved.

No part of this publication may be reproduced in whole or in part, or stored in a
retrieval system, or transmitted in any form or by any means, electronic, mechanical,
photocopying, recording, or otherwise, without written permission of the publisher.
For information regarding permission, write to Scholastic Inc., Attention: Permissions
Department, 557 Broadway, New York, NY 10012.

Published by Scholastic Inc.
90 Old Sherman Turnpike, Danbury, CT 06816.

SCHOLASTIC and associated logos are trademarks and/or registered trademarks of
Scholastic Inc.

ISBN 0-439-72196-2

First Scholastic Printing, July 2005

May and her little brother
Max joined Ash and Pikachu on
their Pokémon journey.

The friends walked through the woods for a long time.

"Can we stop for lunch?" May asked. "I am so hungry!"

"No way!" said Max. "I want to find some Pokémon first."

"We can stop for a quick lunch,"
Ash said. "Then we will look for
Pokémon."

"Yay!" said May and Max.
But there was a problem. All of
their food was gone!

"Pika!" cried Pikachu. Its can
of Pokémon food was empty, too!

"I wish my old friend Brock was here," Ash said. "He knows a lot about Pokémon. And he knows a lot about cooking, too!"

Not far away, Team Rocket
watched the hungry friends.
Jessie, James, and Meowth
were always trying to steal Pikachu.
"Hey look," Meowth said.
"Something's happening!"

Max found a cookie in his pack.
A Pokémon swooped down
before Max could take a bite.
It stole the cookie and flew over
to a tree!

"A Taillow stole my cookie!"
Max yelled.

Ash looked up the Taillow
in his Pokédex.

"Taillow can be fierce," said the
computer. "These flying Pokémon
will not back down in a fight."

"Give us back that cookie!"
May yelled.

"Wait," Ash said. "This tree is
full of fruit. Pikachu, help us knock
down some of that fruit."

15

Zap! Pikachu shocked the trees.
A flock of Taillow flew out!
"I think they are going to
attack!" Max cried.

"Pikachu, Thunderbolt!" Ash yelled.
Pikachu zapped the Taillow.
They fell to the ground.
Then they got
right back up!

The leader of the Taillow
attacked Pikachu.

Pikachu did its best. But it could
not beat the Taillow.

"Taillow are very fierce fighters,"
Ash said.

The Taillow flock joined the attack.

Ash did not know what to do.

Suddenly a Forretress joined the fight!

"Forretress,
Explosion!" a voice
cried.

Boom! Smoke
filled the woods.
The Taillow flock
flew away.

The smoke
cleared. Ash saw
his friend Brock
standing there.

"Thanks, Brock," Ash said. "Your Forretress saved the day."

"Are you really a good cook?" May asked Brock. "Because we could use some lunch!"

"Sure," Brock said. He looked in his pack.

"My sandwiches are gone!" Brock cried.

"I bet the Taillow ate them," May said. "They ate our food, too."

"No problem," Brock said. "I can stir up some stew."

MANVILLE PUBLIC LIBRARY
MANVILLE, NJ 08835

But Team Rocket was stirring up a plan.

"Let's get the Taillow to do our dirty work for us," Meowth said.

MANVILLE PUBLIC LIBRARY
MANVILLE, NJ 08835

Team Rocket had
Brock's sandwiches.
They fed them to
the hungry Taillow

"You can have some more,"
Meowth told the Taillow. "But first
you have to bring us Pikachu!"

The leader of the
Taillow challenged
Pikachu to a fight.
Taillow and
Pikachu faced off.

Zap! Pikachu shocked Taillow.
Swoop! Taillow flew down.

It picked up Pikachu. Then Taillow
dropped Pikachu in the river!

"You have to end the battle," Brock told Ash. "Taillow will not back down."

Ash threw out a Poké Ball. A light zapped Taillow. The Poké Ball closed.

"I caught a Taillow!" Ash cried.

But the battle was not over.
The rest of the Taillow flock wanted
to fight Pikachu, too.
   Ash's Taillow tried to talk them
out of it.

"Give up, Taillow!"
Meowth called.

"That is right," said Jessie.
"These Taillow are our very own
fierce fighting force!"

"They will do anything for
sandwiches," added James.

29

"Hey!" May yelled. "I wanted those sandwiches!" She threw out a Poké Ball. Torchic popped out.

But May forgot to give Torchic a command.

The little Fire
Pokémon ran
into a rock.

Jessie laughed. "Taillow,
attack!"

The Taillow swooped down.
Ding! A bell rang.
"My stew is ready," Brock said.
"Come and get it, Taillow."

The Taillow stopped the attack.
They ate the stew instead.

There was enough stew for everybody . . . except Team Rocket. Pikachu sent them blasting off with a Thundershock.

Finally, the Taillow flock
ate their fill.
They flew away.

Ash's Taillow said good-bye
to its friends.

Ash wanted to get moving, too.

"Catching a Taillow was fun," Ash said. "Let's go look for more Pokémon!"

"Hold on, Ash," Brock said. "We have to do the dishes first."

Ash smiled. "It's good to have you back, Brock," he said.

"Friends should always stick together," said Brock.

Who's That Flying Pokémon?

See page 45 or your *Flying Pokédex* for the answer.

Which One Is Different?

Two of the Pokémon in each row are part of an Evolution chain. One Pokémon does not evolve at all. Can you pick out the Pokémon in each row that does not evolve into or from another Pokémon?

1. Zubat™   Gligar™   Pidgey™

2. Ho-Oh™   Jumpluff™   Masquerain™

3. Zapdos™   Swablu™   Ninjask™

4.

Spearow™

Doduo™

Delibird™

5.

Wingull™

Mantine™

Pidgeotto™

6.

Ledyba™

Hoppip™

Tropius™

7.

Lugia™

Natu™

Skiploom™

39

Check page 45, your *Flying Pokédex,* or your *Ultimate Sticker Book* for the answers.

Name That Beak

Can you tell who these Flying Pokémon are by just looking at each one's beak?

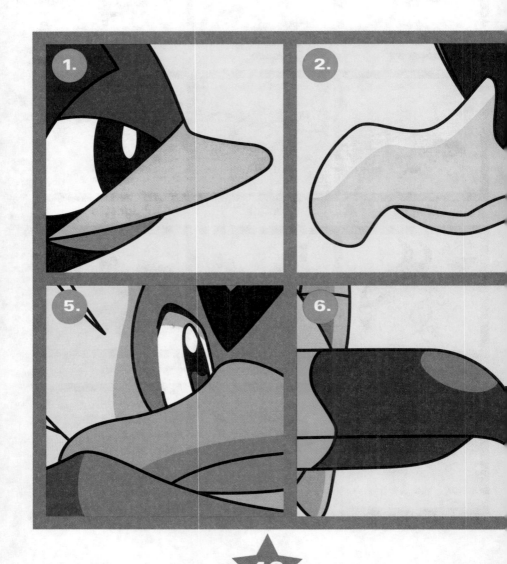

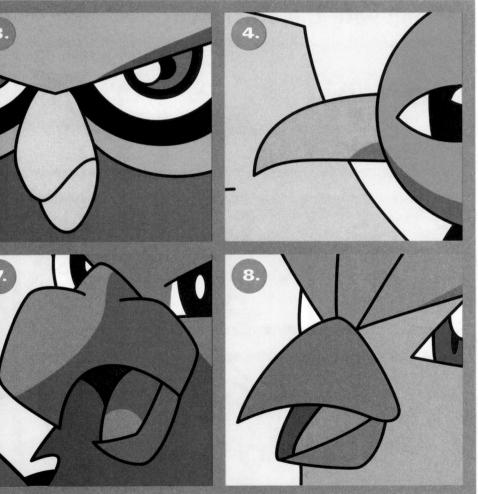

41

Check page 45 or your *Flying Pokédex* for the answers.

Alphabet Attack!

In each row, two of the Flying Pokémon have names that begin with the same letter. The other one does not. Can you pick out the Pokémon that does *not* belong with the other two?

Check page **45** or your
Flying Pokédex for the answers.

Flying Pokémon Jokes

What do you get when you cross a Taillow with a Charizard?

Hot wings!

Why did Ash tie a clock on his Pidgeot's back?

Because he wanted to see time fly!

What kind of books does Hoothoot like to read?

Hoot-dunits!

Why did Ash wash out his Swellow's mouth with soap?

Because it was using fowl language!

What did Brock say when he met the Dodrio?

Hello, hello, hello!

What did Officer Jenny say to the bad Articuno?

Freeze!